One Hundred Christmases

———

One Hundred Christmases

A Novella

Edward L. Woodyard

Three Lions Rampant

New York

By Edward L. Woodyard

One Hundred Christmases

Book Cover: Austin Nelson
Book Design: Swan Graphics

Print Book ISBN: 979-8-9998509-0-4
Ebook ISBN: 979-8-999509-1-1

Library of Congress Control Number: 2025917538

For My Family

Past – Present – Future

Christmas One

On Christmas Eve, when Franz Hartmann was ten years old, his grandfather presented him with a wooden angel he had whittled from a fallen branch of an oak tree that had been struck by lightning behind their home in Bavaria. Franz's grandfather said the wooden angel was to remind Franz of his boyhood Christmases when he placed it atop his first Christmas tree in America. The year was 1872.

"Thank you for the wooden angel, Opa."

"You should thank the dream of a little child born in Bethlehem many hundreds of years ago. And remember, Franz, it is not Christkindl, but a special angel that will be there with you at Christmas, to watch, embrace and protect you, as well as everyone you love."

Franz held the wooden angel in his hands. "Be careful of its wings," his grandfather told him, "Without wings, an angel can't fly from heaven to earth."

"Or to the top of the Christmas tree. The angel looks so real, Opa."

"Real angels give off light, Franz."

"Do you think it will ever be real?"

"Show it love and it will glow. Love will make it real."

"Does it have a name?"

"What do you think its name should be?"

"Gabriel. I could name it for the angel who came to Mary in Nazareth."

"Or maybe it will be something different. It might even name itself when the time is right. But for now, there is a name already on it." His grandfather pointed to the back of the wooden angel's robe where he had carved Franz's name and the year.

Franz smiled when he saw the engraving. His grandfather then helped

Franz place the wooden angel atop the family Christmas tree, hoisting him under his arms. Opa wondered out loud what would happen to the angel one hundred years from now, if it were to last that long. Would it still reign atop a Christmas tree?

When his son Johann took down the Christmas tree at the end of Epiphany, Opa wrapped the wooden angel in a cloth sack for safe passage on the steamship which would take Franz and his parents across the Atlantic Ocean to Baltimore. He told Franz the angel would protect them on the long journey that lay ahead.

As the family bid "Auf Weidersehen" for a last time, love transformed into memory – silent, endless, undeniable.

Aboard the steamship, Franz thought of his grandfather at home in Bavaria and unwrapped the wooden angel from its cloth sack. He felt the smooth folds in the angel's robe and touched the fine detail in the carved face and wings. His mother asked if Franz had yet thought of a name, to which he answered, "Not yet, Mama. Maybe I'll name it after Opa before he becomes an angel. Or after King Ludwig."

"Or after the American king, President Ulysses," his mother suggested.

"Or perhaps the angel is not a him and I can name it Marie Luise after you, Mama."

"Like Opa, I too hope not to be an angel for a very long time."

"There's already a name on it," said Franz's father. "So for now, let's be happy with that name since Christmas is several months away. And let us hope too that the current namesake continues to act like an angel until we get to Missouri."

Several weeks later, the steamship docked in Baltimore. After Johann Hartmann disembarked with his wife and son, he helped them cross a cobblestone road to the terminal of the Baltimore and Ohio Railroad, where they boarded a steam railway for a three-day bench ride to Cincinnati.

Through the train window, Franz showed the wooden angel the passing landscape of its new country. When Franz almost dropped it, his father held open the cloth sack, saying "We should put it away, Franz. We want to keep it safe."

"It's not fragile like glass or porcelain, Papa," answered Franz. "It was why Opa made it of oak so it would last one hundred Christmases."

Johann Hartmann told his son that the figure was not only an archangel, but also an oak angel. "Oak is a symbol of strength and faith. The strength to be found in faith – and the faith to be found in being strong."

He then explained how the ancient Hebrews considered oak sacred because it was under an oak tree that Abraham provided hospitality to God and two of his angels, who were disguised as travelers. "Travelers just like us, Papa."

Johann Hartmann told his son how some pagan tribes in Europe worshipped oak as a symbol of their supreme God. "Oak stands for endurance, fortitude, loyalty, and reliability. The oak tree is a German national symbol, Franz."

"But we are Americans now, Papa."

"That does not mean we lose our heritage. But yes, we are Americans now."

"American oaks."

Once in Cincinnati, the Hartmann family boarded a sternwheeler which took them down the Ohio River then up the Mississippi River, to conclude another ten days of travel at Hannibal, Missouri. There they were to be met by Marie Luise's brother Mattias Trachsel and then ride one more day in a horse-drawn wagon to a small settlement named Palmyra where Mattias had settled several years earlier and cleared forest land for a large farm and homestead.

However, Mattias was not at the wharf in Hannibal to meet them. When neither a room in a boarding house was available nor lodging at an inn, the Hartmann family was offered shelter in the carriage room of a livery stable at a far end of town. That night, Franz held onto the wooden angel as he slept on straw, the irony of the moment not lost on either him or his parents.

Christmas Two

Johann Hartmann completed the four walls of a log cabin in time for Thanksgiving, a custom new to his family but quickly cherished as a tradition to celebrate not only the American family, but also America as family. Mattias shot a wild turkey for the feast which included his wife and their five children, as well as the Hartmanns and three other families from Palmyra.

Johann and Mattias finished thatching the roof of the log cabin a week before Marie Luise insisted that Christmas be celebrated in their new cabin, and for all who could, to please attend a Christmas dinner of venison and pheasant. She said Johann and Franz would position a Christmas tree against a far wall, away from the fieldstone fireplace and a potential of sparks igniting it. "We welcome everyone into our home. No one should be alone at Christmas."

Johann and Franz trudged through a foot of snow with a sled and ax to chop down a young fir tree in a grove of conifers one-half mile from their homestead. They decorated their first Christmas tree in America with dried fruits, fresh apples, strings of berries, ribbons, cookies, pieces of candy and dried leaves.

Its crowning touch was the wooden angel Franz retrieved from its cloth sack and placed with great care and celebration on the top bough of the fir tree. Johann explained how angels symbolized good tidings from the Heavenly Father. "Since angels appeared high in the sky at the first Christmas, people placed angels high on the top of their trees to rejoice in the birth of Jesus."

As Marie Luise arranged small candles in tin cups on the sturdiest tree branches, Franz thought of his grandfather in Bavaria, and of absent family and friends. He then led the singing of "Silent Night" in its original German so they could sing all verses of the Christmas carol.

On Christmas Day after church services, the Hartmann cabin teemed with laughter and feasting, as well as frequent toasts with lager and applejack. Small presents from Kris Kringle were spread on a table and shared among many, followed by games of charades and blindman's bluff, all of which concluded with more singing and sweet stuffs.

Franz waited until the guests left for their homes before presenting Johann and Marie Luise with his gift to them. He asked them to follow a string tied to a bough which led out the door to a clearing beyond the woodpile.

Stacked neatly were three hundred red cedar roof shingles Franz had axed and planed so the cabin would now have a solid roof to hold off rain and snow, as well as to keep the cabin interior dry, especially its dirt floor. Surprised at Franz's generosity and ingenuity, his parents wondered how he had found the wherewithal to accomplish such a task. He told of finding red cedars on limestone bluffs and glades nearby, then of sneaking away after school lessons and farm chores to hand-split the shakes with a froe ax and mallet. He said he learned the craft by watching and helping Opa back in Bavaria.

While delighted with their Christmas gift, the Hartmanns however noticed an eerie light flicker through the open cabin door. A candle flame had ignited a tree branch.

Johann and Franz rushed into the house to douse the fire with water from a bucket. Relieved that the thatched roof hadn't also been ignited, they hugged each other. Johann then lifted Franz up by his shoulders to examine the wooden angel at the top of the Christmas tree.

"All is good, Papa. The Christmas Angel is not charred or blackened by smoke."

Johann replied, "Franz, you have given Opa's angel its name."

He then said that he did not want their first Christmas in America to be remembered with a scorched and fallen angel, thus forever marking it in his mind as a time of distress and tribulation.

Despite his hope, that upheaval arrived with the spring thaw, when Marie Luise died during a smallpox epidemic and later, when his crops failed that autumn, Johann was forced to leave his son in Palmyra with Mattias while he sought better fortune as a miner of silver ore in the Rocky Mountains of the Colorado Territory.

Christmas Six

Franz Hartmann did not see his father again for another four years. Correspondence between them was sporadic – until Franz received a small package before Christmas that did not contain a ribboned gift, but instead held an envelope with a railway ticket to Denver, three $20 gold coins wrapped in a linen handkerchief, and a letter signed "your father, John Hartman."

Franz was mystified by the reasons for the package's contents and the letter's signature. The letter requested Franz to join his father in the new federal state of Colorado. He was not quite sure of his father's seemingly sudden intentions, or of the source of his seemingly sudden wealth.

Franz had matured into a responsible young man under the tutelage of his uncle Mattias, continuing his formal lessons, assuming obligations for farm crops and animals, and assisting in a livery. He centered his life on family, church, school, work, and community. Franz commented that girls now noticed him in a different manner, with his uncle Mattias reassuring him that such attention would be the least of his problems.

Summers passed and winter meant Christmas, Franz's favorite time of year. With his observant Christmas Angel perched atop the tree, Franz welcomed those times of food, caroling and joy. Despite an absence of family members and old friends, more revelers were greeted and received. New memories were made while others were refreshed, especially when more children added hand-made ornaments and decorations to the Christmas tree each yuletide season.

And in its silence, the Christmas Angel held its place of prominence overlooking the smiles and laughter until the tree was taken outside at Epiphany and Franz would rub the Christmas Angel with beeswax before placing it again in its cloth sack, wishing it a long good night until the next December – which would find them both in Denver.

After his Christmas in Palmyra, Franz packed a leather satchel with clothes and the Christmas Angel, prayed at his mother's gravesite, and said good-bye to his aunt and cousins before Mattias drove him by wagon to Hannibal from where he boarded a railway to Kansas City. After first sending his father a telegram to say that he was on his way, Franz presented his ticket and rode the Kansas Pacific Railway to Denver.

His father was certainly doing well, Franz thought; his two-day passage across the Great Plains was in a Pullman car. Sitting with and dining among some fancy fellow passengers, Franz felt humbled by his modest clothes. He hesitated to discuss himself and preferred to watch the passing countryside out the window. Nevertheless, he did study how these people interacted with each other, particularly how they held a teacup and sliced meat with a knife then brought it to their mouths with a fork. He sensed he would need to know these lessons where he was going. He wondered if his father was now one of them.

When the railway terminated in Denver, Franz recognized his father standing on the platform. However, he was dressed in a dark suit with a gold chain swung between two vest pockets and he sported a bowler on his head.

But he was not alone: a woman in a long, ruffled dress and a wide-brimmed hat with flowing plumes stood next to him. When his father opened his arms to welcome an excited Franz, the woman cautioned him to stand up and just extend an arm to his son, offering a firm handshake instead of a warm hug. When the woman held out her gloved hand to Franz, she introduced herself as Mother Hortense and referred to Franz as Frank. She insisted now that they were among proper American society, both he and his father possess anglicized names. As a driver helped them into a two-horse sleigh outside the railway station, Frank Hartman was born.

Christmas Seven

Frank Hartman was introduced into a world as foreign to him as Egypt was to the Israelites. Excelling in his academic studies thankfully guided him through the pratfalls of unfamiliar surroundings, helping him navigate the demands and peculiarities of a Denver social circle burgeoning with the newly arrived, his father and stepmother being so duly anointed on the sheer merits of a hefty bank balance. John Hartman had not struck a bonanza of silver in the Colorado mountains above Ute City but one of molybdenite, a mineral critical to harden iron ore into steel. Almost instantly upon settling in Denver, he was snared by a widow whose deceased first husband lost his fortune in a railroad land swindle.

Frank's first Christmas in Denver was notable for one reason: Hortense refused to allow the Christmas Angel on the tree. She said it would distract from the shimmer of the imported glass ornaments which dominated the large pine in the front parlor of their ornate home off Colfax Avenue.

Instead, the Christmas Angel stood watch over Frank while he slept. He left it propped over his bed through the yuletide, then secured it in a dresser drawer after Epiphany to await the next Christmas. Such was his routine for the following three years until he was sent East for college.

Tensions between Frank and his stepmother increased during that time, most notably in the June before he entered Yale, when a census taker asked questions about the residents living in their home, particularly names, ages and birth places. Hortense sternly corrected his father's answers, causing the census taker to line through entries with amended notations: the head of household's name was John, not Johann; his son was Frank, not Franz; both males were from Missouri, not Bavaria. As the census taker left, Frank heard him remark that he doubted if the Roman census taker in Bethlehem experienced similar adjustments with Joseph and Mary.

While studying in New Haven, Frank received a letter from his father prior to his scheduled return home for that Christmas. It stated that Hortense preferred Frank to remain East during the holidays and suggested that Frank seek employment in Boston or New York during the upcoming summer months. Frank then considered a plan to spend the holidays with his mother's family in Palmyra, but decided against that alternative, reluctantly agreeing to his father's request to remain East, for the sake of family harmony. His Christmases were not spent alone; his gift to others was helping the less fortunate through the Salvation Army, with warm clothes and hot meals.

Frank Hartman did not return to Colorado for another six years, when he received a telegram in New York that his father was himself prepared to be an angel. Frank arrived in Denver by passenger train four days later, in time to deliver his father's eulogy. However, as he disembarked at the railway station, a chambermaid from the household instructed him that his stepmother had reserved a room for him at the Windsor Hotel.

After the funeral, Frank returned to the hotel where the same chambermaid waited in the lobby with a steamer trunk. The chambermaid told him that as his father lay dying, Hortense ordered the staff to clean out all drawers and closets in the guest quarters where Frank had stayed during his visits to see his father.

Frank quickly searched the steamer trunk for the Christmas Angel, but it wasn't there. He asked the chambermaid if she remembered it from the dresser in his bedroom.

At first, she thought it had been discarded, but then recalled another chambermaid named Katerina Wolters had taken it from the trash, saying that since the wooden angel was handmade, she preferred it to those fancy-schmancy glass ornaments in the front parlor. When Frank asked about Katerina, the chambermaid said she was no longer in the employ of the Hartman household, remarking that she quit when Mr. Hartman died and had eloped to Wyoming with a stableman named Patrick Conlon.

Frank thanked the chambermaid and handed her a generous tip for her troubles. She curtsied slightly and left the hotel.

After he and the steamer trunk boarded the next train to New York, Frank knew his childhood Christmases would now remain moments not to be relived again. He wanted the Christmas Angel to have a good home, with people who cherished it as much as he did. And he wished their Christmas memories with the Christmas Angel would be as rewarding.

Upon his return to New York, Frank received a letter from an attorney declaring his father's estate had been awarded solely to his widow Hortense.

Despite its worth, Frank's new life possessed greater value. He had fallen in love with a woman at his Manhattan office named Helen Armstrong and that Christmas Eve, he proposed marriage to her while ice skating on the frozen lake in Central Park. Together, they created new Christmas memories, especially after their two sons were born.

Later, during the Great Depression, when he was asked by his grandchildren about his childhood Christmases, Frank Hartman showed them a tintype of Opa and told them the story of the hand-whittled Christmas Angel which guided and protected him and his family for all those years when they first settled in America. Helen reminded Frank the Christmas Angel still looked after them, only now it also guided and protected another family, last known to be somewhere in Wyoming in the 1890s.

Or so they hoped.

Christmas Fifteen

Patrick and Katerina Conlon had journeyed to a Shoshone village within the Wind River Reservation as Christian missionaries. Patrick had been a Jesuit seminarian until he realized he was a freethinker who loved Katerina and horses as much as he did Jesus and his teachings.

He and Katerina settled at Fort Washakie, the oldest community on the reservation and named for Chief Washakie, who negotiated the treaty establishing it. He was buried there, as was Lewis and Clark's Shoshone guide, Sacajawea. Buffalo Soldiers, U.S. cavalrymen of African descent, were garrisoned there to maintain order in the expanding frontier.

The Conlons lived the life they preached, one of doing unto others as they would have others do unto them. Their small congregation incorporated the culture and demography of the area which included Shoshones, pioneers and soldiers. All helped build a chapel on a hill within sight of the fort, holding services and praying as they laid a foundation, erected walls and placed a steeple atop its roof, each Sunday praising the Lord and giving thanks for God's glory.

During the congregation's celebration upon completion of the chapel, Katerina gave birth to a boy. Like every father gazing at his first child, Patrick Conlon believed he held the hope of the world in his arms, that maybe now God and nature might finally have got it right. Even with desires and wishes, he and Katerina couldn't agree on what to call their newborn son so they delayed his baptism until such time they agreed on a name.

Snow and Christmas soon followed the baby's birth. After Patrick and Katerina placed a small blue spruce in the center of the unfurnished chapel on Christmas Day, parishioners adorned the tree with personal decorations and mementos. A Shoshone girl draped a long garland she had triple-beaded, while pioneer families scattered hand-sewn cloth ornaments and beribboned cookies onto boughs. One soldier hung braided horsehair figurines onto branches while another secured several leather straps adorned with brass buttons. With Patrick's help, Katerina carefully placed at the top of the tree the Christmas Angel she rescued in Denver.

Katerina likened the Christmas Angel to a favorite Christmas carol, "Angels We Have Heard On High," saying it was the Gloria in Excelsis Deo angel. "Glory in the highest," she said, "the highest on the tree." She would have called the angel Gloria except another name was inscribed on it.

When a Shoshone boy then asked about the name on the wooden angel, Patrick instead told the story of the birth of the Christ child and the hope the baby named Jesus gave to the world at the time, and still gave to the world. He stated how an angel named Gabriel told the Virgin Mary she would have such a child, to which the Shoshone boy said the wooden angel should be named Gabriel.

Katerina pulled her husband aside to say there was already a name on it: Franz Hartmann. She said he was probably related to the Hartman family they used to work for – except that Hortense was no saintly being. Katerina whispered to Patrick, "The mistress was more like a fallen angel, the devil incarnate."

While the young Shoshone boy's suggested name of Gabriel wasn't appropriate for the wooden angel, the Conlons thought it would be a perfect name for their angelic newborn child. Patrick then baptized his son under the Christmas tree, with water the Shoshone boy had scooped into a bucket from a nearby stream.

But not everyone was happy with the symbols and rituals of Christmas. A chief of the Shoshone tribe refused to comment on the christening of the child because he said it was too young to make such decisions; however, he proclaimed the wooden angel to be a false idol. He then declared the presence of another false idol, the Christmas tree. "That's religion," he said. "That's not God."

Regardless, the congregation sang carols and said final prayers before heading to their homes, tepees and barracks to await a visit from Saint Nicholas. Later that night, the Christmas tree caught fire, a sentry at the fort alerting soldiers who raced to pull the burning tree from the chapel, then used blankets to smother the flames and save the building.

When Katerina searched the scorched tree the following morning, she couldn't find the wooden angel and feared it had been consumed by the fire. However, as Patrick examined the smoke damage to the chapel's floor and ceiling, he found the wooden angel floating face down in the bucket of water used to baptize their son, as if it had wanted to baptize itself in its descent from the treetop. Katerina called it a small miracle, then tucked the Christmas Angel under the same blanket which swathed young Gabriel. She and Patrick recognized the destruction of the Christmas tree as a warning they needed to heed.

In the spring, the Conlon family loaded a Conestoga wagon and moved east across the Northern Plains of Nebraska and Iowa to central Wisconsin to join Katerina's sister and husband, where Patrick could labor in the timber mills. As they traveled toward the safety of a new home and the mystery of a next chapter in life, Patrick remarked to Katerina their journey was like that of Mary and Joseph when they took their baby into Egypt to flee forces which feared them.

Christmas Twenty-Six

For someone who owned a timber mill, Katerina's brother-in-law lived in a residence built with competitive material: a two-story Victorian house recently constructed of bricks fired from clay on the property. The Conlon family would live in a log cabin which had been Lena and Lars Bolstad's first home and where their two young children Isabella and Anders were born.

Katerina and Lena Wolters had lived with their parents in Milwaukee, their father being a brewmeister at Pabst Best Select. Both sisters worked the brewery saloon and met their eventual husbands there, both of whom had traveled together from New York City, one from Ireland and the other from Norway, Patrick teaching English to Lars while they worked as deckhands up the Hudson River, through the Erie Canal and across the Great Lakes to Milwaukee. Katerina followed Patrick to the mining camps of Colorado to cook and proselytize, while Lena helped Lars as a cutler and nurse in the lumber camps one hundred miles northwest of Milwaukee, where more than one lumberjack wondered why Lars spoke English with a brogue.

Gabriel was walking by the time he celebrated his first Christmas in Wisconsin. When Patrick and Katerina showed Isabella and Anders the Christmas Angel they brought with them from Wyoming, Isabella asked to hold it, but then raced it around the house over her head as she attempted to have it soar into heaven to join other angels already there. A fortunate catch by her father Lars saved the Christmas Angel from injury to its head and wings.

While the Christmas Angel would now need to be placed out of reach of curious fingers, that didn't mean a young child couldn't still place it atop the Christmas tree. Gabriel held onto the wooden angel as Patrick lifted him to do the honors. Until his son became too heavy to raise with both hands, Patrick hoisted Gabriel every yuletide to position the Christmas Angel in its place of honor. Eventually, Gabriel would climb onto his father's shoulders to perform the tradition – until he became so tall he could do it himself, despite paternal guidance.

Gabriel's memories of the holidays stayed fresh every year, the central place for song and prayer being the music room of the Bolstad home which also served as a worship house since no parishioner had yet to erect a church building from the wood planks and joists being generated at the timber mill. Lars cited a lack of time due to fulfilling orders for boards and beams being sent east, west and south as an excuse to prefer the Bolstad home for prayer services. Being practical as well, most in the area accepted this arrangement, asking why erect a church building when there was already a perfectly good worship hall being offered for the same purpose.

The Bolstad Christmas Eve service was a union of Presbyterian and Lutheran rituals, with the top of an already hewn fir, spruce or pine reimagined each season into the annual Christmas tree. Over the years, Gabriel and his Bolstad cousins searched the lumber yard of felled trees before they were limbed and bucked, pulling that year's chosen tree home on a sled or cart. Upon positioning the tree by the music room's front window, the congregation decorated it during Advent with store-bought trinkets and hand-made ornaments, most being woven straw, cut-out paper snowflakes, sugar cookies and painted pinecones.

When Isabella created a papier-mâché star for the top of the tree, the Christmas Angel enjoyed a new perch: on the roof of a miniature stable Gabriel and Anders built at the mill which featured painted clay Nativity figurines shipped from France. Content as guardian of the Baby Jesus and the Magi, the Christmas Angel oversaw the festivity and wonder of each holiday season: the wafts of fresh lefse and glogg, the sight of children dancing a jig and the sound of a fiddle and squeezebox playing carols. Those assembled were allowed to open one present before going home to await Saint

Nicholas, but not before Gabriel began another tradition for the lumberjack families: a moment of silence and thanks. He said the Christmas Angel wanted everyone to stop, be quiet and just listen. "The angel wants us to feel all the love in the room."

Everyone hushed as they settled around the Christmas tree until the younger children could no longer restrain their anticipation and ripped open presents, with others soon to follow. They all knew love was always in the room in every home at Christmastime.

Then war disturbed the quiet and interrupted that love. When the battleship U.S.S. *Maine* blew up in Havana harbor, Lars and Patrick volunteered for a Wisconsin infantry unit sent to Cuba. Despite having survived the cavalry charge up San Juan Hill and then welcoming the war's conclusion within several months, they remained garrisoned in the Caribbean until the formal signing of a peace treaty in Paris.

Gabriel sensed the Christmas Angel dreaded it would witness a somber and restrained Christmas that year; the absence of men around the tree let wives and mothers fear the worst for their soldiers, from both enemy bullets and typhoid fever. When a troop train arrived in Milwaukee in mid-December, quiet wasn't needed for anyone to feel the love in the room as Lars and Patrick arrived home in time for a Christmas jig, a glass of glogg and many an embrace from family and friends.

However, the joy and gratitude of that Christmas was short-lived. Lars Bolstad contracted typhoid on the troop ship home and died before the end of Epiphany. Lena then learned Lars had placed the business in receivership before he left for Cuba and the mill would be seized from her by creditors if Patrick didn't assume control of the operation. However, Patrick proved unable to manage the timber mill profitably, and against the wishes of his wife and sister-in-law, he signed over majority ownership of the business to a competing lumber operation. Patrick soon realized his mistake but could do nothing to reverse fate.

The following winter, a teenaged Gabriel found his father under a seventy-foot blue spruce, his ax in his calloused hands. How could he have let a tree land on him? He was too experienced and knowledgeable about felling to allow that mistake. What had happened? Did something spook him? A hunter? A deer? A sudden wind? The town doctor ruled Patrick's death an accident caused by an act of God.

Gabriel soon realized his father had been unversed in the matters of commerce. He had no bank account and no last will and testament. Lena told everyone not to worry, that God would provide, but her sister Katerina wasn't so sure.

Soon after the turn of the century, Lena sold the brick Victorian house to a bank to cover debts incurred during prior mismanagement of the mill, thus forcing the congregation to build a church nearby. The house sale prompted Lena and her two children to move into their original cabin with Katerina and Gabriel.

When Gabriel and Anders learned their jobs at the timber mill had been eliminated, their Wolters grandfather offered to obtain each a job at the brewery in Milwaukee; instead, they enlisted in the American Expeditionary Forces. The war in Europe magnetized young men seeking adventure and glory. Paris awaited – and so did French girls.

Christmas of 1917 first found Katerina and Lena in the newly built church sanctuary, praying and singing carols – with both hoping their sons were safe and protected. The two widowed sisters returned to the cabin after the Christmas Eve service and went to bed. There was neither a fire to warm the hearth nor a tree and presents to warm the heart. The Christmas Angel remained in its cloth sack that Christmas, on a shelf in the stable, above a cow, two hogs and several chickens while a mule munched hay strewn in a manger.

Christmas Forty-Seven

The war to end all wars did anything but. Gabriel and Anders fought the Kaiser in the trenches of northern Europe. Gabriel wrote one letter home, telling of a Christmas Day truce where carols were sung across a battlefield in both English and German, the lyrics in different languages but the tunes the same. He then asked his mother to tell his Aunt Lena that Anders had died from mustard gas poisoning in the days after Christmas and was buried in Belgium. In her delirium at the loss, Lena remarked to her sister, "Flanders and Anders. They rhyme. Maybe someone will write a poem."

Although an armistice was signed in November 1918, Gabriel remained on active duty in Europe. While Katerina, Lena and Isabella waited in the original cabin for Gabriel's return, they were snowed in that December and celebrated Christmas by placing the Christmas Angel on the stone mantelpiece and singing "Angels We Have Heard On High."

Yet the weight of another blizzard caused the cabin's roof planks to collapse inward, forcing a decision. Despite townspeople's generous offers of accommodations and lodging in homes or at the mill, Lena and Isabella moved to Milwaukee to live with Lena's father and work in the brewery – while Katerina accepted an offer as a domestic in Chicago, executing duties she knew – and didn't mind performing. The wife of the bank owner who bought the Bolstad house arranged for her to obtain the housekeeping position.

A grateful Katerina rode a locomotive train south two hundred miles, accompanied by a steamer trunk of clothes and prized possessions. Christmas would come to Chicago too, she told herself, although she now had a doubt in her mind. In her haste to pack, she forgot the Christmas Angel, leaving it perched on the stone mantelpiece in Wisconsin.

While Katerina Conlon had no way to notify Gabriel in Europe about geographic changes within the family, she trusted he would figure it out in due time, same as he had done with most things in his adult life. She surmised he would most likely travel back to the place from where he started. Townspeople would be certain to let him know the disturbances within the family, but Katerina also knew Gabriel would realize, with family gone, his home there would be no more. She hoped he'd join her in Chicago where she could help him start his life over, forget the war as best as he could, and try to enjoy the pleasures of life again. She kept a candle lit in a window of her two leased rooms overlooking a small park so he wouldn't be forgotten.

A mother's intuition proved correct. Gabriel returned from war and learned what happened once he got to Wisconsin. The proprietor of the general store provided details and the banker's wife gave him an address in Chicago. Still in uniform, he visited his father in the cemetery and then found the Christmas

Angel among the ruins of the original cabin, still on the stone mantelpiece where his mother had placed it the prior Christmas. Its face was dirty and its wings streaked with soot, but he knew lemon oil and beeswax would restore his guardian angel to its pristine glory. Unable to find its cloth sack amid the debris, Gabriel wrapped it in a hand towel, placed it in his pack and trekked the next eight days through forests and fields to Chicago. For Gabriel, the spring air was filled with hope and promise, an absolution from fear and death.

A tired Gabriel arrived at the apartment building in Chicago at dusk, curious about a candle lit in a second story window. Katerina greeted her son with never-too-many hugs then fed him, regaling him about the wealthy family for whom she worked and displaying her maid's uniform, with its lace collar, apron and cap. Gabriel told his mother their memories reaffirmed they hadn't lost their family, saying only that their lives had been redefined and shifted. They were happy to be with each other, no matter the time or place.

Katerina dressed Gabriel in a castoff suit from her employer and within a week he signed on with the Chicago Surface Lines as a trolley conductor on an electrified streetcar. Among his regular passengers was a young nurse who finally told him her name was Rose Salerno. After she gave him permission to call on her at her hospital residence, he spent a week's wages on a corsage and dinner for two at a lakefront restaurant which featured white tablecloths and a violinist. Their eyes told them all they needed to know. Nothing more was necessary except set a date for their wedding. Gabriel Conlon remembered his father had told him love would reveal to him the man he was meant to be, just as it had for himself when he met Gabriel's mother.

Gabriel and Katerina's first Christmas in Chicago was steeped in an anticipation multiplied in proportion to the city population. They said they wouldn't let their financial problems and lack of cash interfere with the excitement and joy of the Christmas season.

Gabriel had spied a thicket of fir trees at a northern terminus of the trolley line, its land being cleared for a housing development. He borrowed a hatchet and brought home a small evergreen tied to the streetcar. A regular passenger who wore three-piece suits congratulated Gabriel on his ingenuity, saying he'd noticed his dedication to responsibility and asked Gabriel if he'd allow him to arrange an interview for him with the railroad. Gabriel said yes; there was no hurt in it.

On Christmas Eve, Katerina arrived home early in zero-degree weather and snow flurries, but she was warmed by seeing a Christmas tree in its stand by the front window, waiting to be trimmed. She felt the renewal the holidays bring. She also carried a box of electric Christmas lights, a gift from her employer, and a bag with almonds, raisins and Madeira to make glogg.

Rose met Gabriel at the trolley barn, holding a panettone she had baked. They hurried toward his apartment, only stopping at a cigar store and then for impromptu caroling with some neighbors outside the building.

Katerina kissed them both when they entered the apartment and rubbed their hands to warm them. The new electric lights were unboxed and the ornaments ready to be hung. Gabriel excused himself to change out of his conductor's uniform while Rose was introduced to glogg. She noticed the Christmas Angel on a table.

Katerina told about it having been thrown out when she and Patrick worked in Denver, how a spelling of that family's name was engraved in the bottom folds of the robe. Rose didn't understand how something so beautiful could be discarded, saying for her it was like seeing a Christmas tree curbside in early January. Something which had brought so much happiness to so many was tossed aside when its purpose was over. Katerina agreed about the tree but then remarked how Christmas ornaments such as the Christmas Angel remain timeless, that they help assure families of their traditions and create an annual holiday magic.

Katerina handed Rose the oak angel. She saw its inscription, "Franz Hartmann 1872," and became curious as to whom he was and the importance of that year.

"I've wondered that myself, Rose. Regardless, I admire it. Through everything, the angel has given us luck. Gabriel was named because of it."

Gabriel strung the new electric lights on the tree, questioning what the Christmas Angel would say about them if it could talk.

"Angels don't have to speak," Rose said, "They fly directly to the heart of the matter. They're never too far away so as not to hear you. And they hear you best when you're in prayer or silent thought."

Gabriel then said angels wouldn't hear them right now because they would be toasting with glogg. As the Christmas tree shined with its new electric lights, Gabriel placed the Christmas Angel at its top. Katerina told Rose how Gabriel first performed that duty as a baby, about when his father lifted him up and made sure he held on tight so the angel could find its special place.

As Rose admired the angel, under its gaze Gabriel placed a small rectangular package, attached to which was Rose's name on a tag. He told her she could open it later, that the tradition in Wisconsin had let everyone open one gift on Christmas Eve before going to church.

Enjoying the panettone after dinner, Rose opened the rectangular package from the tree. It held a single cigar, its red-and-gold foil band embossed with "La Rosa." Rose was confused.

Gabriel explained, "I can't afford a ring right now so please think of this cigar band as a reminder that I promise you something better in the future." Rose was still confused.

But Katerina wasn't. "He's asking you to marry him, Rose. I always said my son was smart." There was no reason on this Christmas Eve for Gabriel to ask for a moment of silence. The love was already in the room for everyone to embrace.

At church that night, Rose removed her woolen gloves and stared proudly at the cigar band on the fourth finger of her left hand. She admired it as if it were encrusted with glittery gems. Someday, Gabriel told her, she would have diamonds and rubies. She answered she would never need them. She already had her jewel. She had him.

Gabriel and Rose married the following summer in the same church. His new position on the 20th Century Limited allowed them to buy a new home in the housing development where he had found their first Christmas tree. When their son Theodore was born a year later, Gabriel smoked the La Rosa cigar in his son's honor, its red-and-gold foil band safe in his wife's jewelry box, beside a shining ruby-and-diamond ring.

Christmas Sixty-Two

For Theo's first Christmas in their new home in Caldwell Heights, Gabriel bought a Christmas tree at a sale to benefit a local chapter of Veterans of Foreign Wars, a patriotic organization he recently joined. Just as his father had done for him, Gabriel hoisted his young son to show him where to place the Christmas Angel on the tree while a pregnant Rose Conlon joined Katerina in singing "Angels We Have Heard On High."

When Theo's sister Patricia was born, their grandmother Katerina moved into their home to help in the care of her two grandchildren. Rose worked nights at a local hospital and Gabriel's position with the railroad kept him away from home for days on end. He was required to write reports about each round trip, which his supervisor then forwarded to the railroad's headquarters in New York City.

Gabriel and Rose felt it was an imposition on Katerina to ask her to be there, a suggestion she resisted. "If you let me help you, you'll help me in return. You don't realize sometimes until it's too late, that by touching the lives of others in a wonderful, positive way, you have made your own life and those of others just as wonderful and positive." Her words reinforced why they preferred living in a small town where they knew most people – and welcomed what they could do to serve others.

The Dust Bowl and Stock Market Crash occurred spontaneously, making many question what they had done to deserve God's wrath and punishment. Through thrift and adaptation to circumstances, Gabriel and his family managed to escape two of the Great Depression's grimmest perils, destitute homelessness and starvation poverty. Both he and Rose held onto their jobs, with his father Patrick's Spanish-American War pension contributing toward food and bills. Christmas gifts were often hand-crafted: Rose knit sweaters and scarves while Katerina baked cakes and breads, and Gabriel refinished an abandoned dining table and chairs found on the street. All three saved nickels and dimes so the two young children could open gifts they desired on Christmas morning: a porcelain-faced doll for Patricia and a toy fire truck for Theo.

In the week before Christmas, when President Franklin Roosevelt had earlier said the only thing to fear was fear itself, Gabriel rode a streetcar into Chicago to purchase the presents his children wanted to open under the tree. On his way to the toy store, he visited his former neighborhood. The place wasn't the same as he remembered. Perhaps what he saw was due to winter weather or maybe neglect caused by a lack of currency. He noticed most landlords no longer maintained their buildings, especially when tenants were threatened with eviction and squatters crowded abandoned rooms. His former apartment building housed immigrants from Eastern and Southern Europe, as well as migrants from the Deep South, all in search of available work in the factories and stockyards within the area.

Amid despair and chaos, Gabriel spied a sign of hope that the Christmas season brings: a snowman in the front yard being made by a carefree and smiling young boy who introduced himself as Reginald Washington.

"And what's your name?" he asked.

"Gabriel Conlon."

"Gabriel, like the angel who told Mary about the birth of the Baby Jesus. Maybe you're my angel. Actually, my mama is. We live right there." He pointed to the same window in which Katerina Conlon had placed a lighted candle to welcome her son home from the war.

"I lived there once too."

Reginald's mother exited the building with seven lumps of coal for the snowman's face. "Don't ask for anymore. People need the coal to heat their stoves."

"Mr. Conlon, this is my mama."

"I'm Pearl Washington. I'm pleased to meet you."

"Mr. Conlon is here to make sure the Baby Jesus is born and Santa

Claus will know about a place that has no chimney to come down, unless it's through the coal chute."

"Times are tough, Reginald," said his mother.

"People have been collecting coal from railroad tracks," Gabriel told the young boy. "They don't know how dangerous that can be for them."

"Since they can get hit by the trains rolling down the tracks."

"Reginald, you do talk. Please excuse my son's imagination."

"I have a son the same age. He too has a vivid imagination," answered Gabriel.

"What's his name?" asked Reginald.

"Theo. It's short for Theodore. His name means a gift of God."

"Mama, why did God make my skin brown?"

"Because God knew that color looked the best on you. God makes people beautiful in all different colors. Except God didn't make green people."

"If God did make people green, then they wouldn't know if they had a booger hanging out of their nose."

Gabriel laughed abruptly while Pearl tried to admonish her son despite her giggling, moving him toward his snowman. Gabriel changed the subject, "Are you ready for Christmas?"

"It's not going to be much of a holiday this year. It's just Reginald and me. My husband's laid up on our farm in Tennessee and I send money home. I work as cleaning help for two families in Evanston and one has me working the afternoon of Christmas Day. Reginald and I got all the decorations put up around our place but no tree. I can't afford it. Maybe I need to believe in a miracle this Christmas, but sometimes with things the way they are, you lose faith."

Gabriel heard her, but said, "I know you will make your Christmas the best you can."

"I hope so. It seems like hope is all we have these days. But hope doesn't feed and clothe us. Merry Christmas all the same."

"And Merry Christmas to you. I need to get back home. It's a pleasure to meet you, Mrs. Washington. And you too, Reginald. I know you've been nice, so Santa will be good to you."

With Reginald busy placing lumps of coal to create the face on his snowman, Pearl Washington whispered to Gabriel, "I'm afraid there won't be any Santa Claus this year. Money and efforts are all going elsewhere."

Gabriel said good-bye and walked three blocks to the toy store, later arriving home on the streetcar with his Christmas shopping done. Rose and Katerina had decorated the downstairs for the family open house on Christmas Eve, when friends and neighbors celebrated the season with music and food. But first, Gabriel had to close the VFW Christmas Tree sale. He saw there was one small fir remaining on the lot which wouldn't be someone's Christmas tree this year, until he remembered someone who might be grateful for it.

With the Christmas Angel adorning yet another wonderful Christmas morning, the Conlon family opened presents, ate homemade panettone and drank hot chocolate. Patricia cradled her new doll; Rose admired her new dining table; Katerina wore her new scarf and mittens; and Gabriel hugged himself in his new sweater.

But of everyone, Theo was the most excited about what Santa Claus had left for him: a toy fire truck with two hoses, two axes, a siren, a steering wheel that turned the front tires, a miniature Dalmatian dog on the front seat and a swivel ladder that cranked to reach a burning upstairs window of a house ablaze, all allowing Theo to pretend he was extinguishing the Great Chicago Fire from sixty years earlier. Gabriel couldn't remember himself ever being as thrilled about a gift as Theo was with his new fire truck, but he hadn't been eight years old in a while.

Christmas dinner would be later that afternoon, in time for Lena and Isabella to arrive from Milwaukee. The delay let Gabriel do one more thing which prompted Theo to ask if he could ride the trolley with his father – and if he could bring his fire truck with them. He promised while his father held on tight to the small fir tree, he would hold on as tight to his favorite gift from Santa Claus.

When the trolley stopped, Gabriel and Theo walked two blocks to find Reginald sitting on the front steps of the apartment building with his arms crossed and his mother trying to resurrect a damaged snowman. Gabriel noticed other children in the yard showing each other what Santa Claus had brought them, all laughing and happy with their new toys and presents.

But not Reginald. He had pushed over his snowman in anger

and frustration. His mother welcomed seeing Gabriel again unexpectedly and to meet Theo. She was delighted with the small fir, saying it was appropriate for a Christmas tree to be put up and decorated on Christmas Day. Gabriel and Pearl Washington carried the tree upstairs while outside Reginald asked Theo if they could play together with his new fire truck so that he could at least have a touch of Christmas. Theo showed him all the moveable parts and how they worked.

In his former apartment, Gabriel felt nostalgic seeing the small fir tree in the corner and told Pearl about the Christmas Angel which was always on top of their tree, and was now in their new home. She said, "The spirit of your Christmas Angel is still here, Mr. Conlon."

Gabriel told her he and Theo needed to get home since family members were due for Christmas dinner. Pearl said she had made a stew and thanked him again for his generosity.

Once outside, Gabriel and Pearl saw their sons playing together with the fire truck, its swivel ladder extended up the front step to rescue people trapped inside a burning building.

"Reginald, Mr. Conlon and his son have to go now. Please give Theo back his fire truck."

"It's mine, Mama. Theo said that Santa Claus had left it for me at his house."

"Dad," said Theo, "I opened it by mistake, without looking at the name tag on it. I didn't notice the present had Reginald's name on it."

"See, Mama, we do have Christmas after all."

"Yes, we do, Reginald. But Mr. Conlon, I can't. . ."

"Thank the Christmas Angel, Mrs. Washington. And Merry Christmas."

Pearl clasped Gabriel's hand as Theo waved good-bye to Reginald and the fire truck. Gabriel put his arm around Theo as they walked the two blocks to the trolley.

Gabriel had been given the greatest Christmas present he could receive. It was not only the one Theo had given Reginald, but the more important one Theo had given his father. Gabriel witnessed a moment parents wish for themselves: when their child becomes a better person than they are.

On the trolley ride home, Theo said he had done what he did because he wanted the Christmas Angel to be real.

While Gabriel wasn't sure what Theo meant by his statement, he knew he couldn't love his son more than he did right then.

Christmas
Seventy-Two

G abriel's position at the railroad inoculated his family from the full effects of the Great Depression. His knowledge of freight routes and maintenance schedules was crucial to transport products and goods across the nation. As his boss liked to say, Gabriel Conlon kept the nation on track. When Rose was promoted to head nurse at the hospital, Theo and Patricia enjoyed their independence during their school years, despite witnessing bread lines and shantytowns when they journeyed into Chicago for Cubs baseball games, school museum trips, and family visits to the Chicago World's Fair.

The Nazis invaded Poland during Theo's first semester at Lake Forest College. He and his roommate Albert Robbins deliberated their fate. If war came to America, they said they would enlist first before being conscripted.

During their junior year of college, fate decided. Three days after the destruction of Pearl Harbor, Theo enlisted in the Marines while Albert returned home to New York City to join the Army. Both would begin basic training in a month.

Theo was allowed to enjoy Christmas at home before reporting for duty. His family knew it would be their last Christmas together for a long time – or perhaps ever again.

Theo accompanied Gabriel to select an evergreen from the VFW Christmas tree lot, Gabriel revealing his son's decision to fellow veterans who then shook Theo's hand and wished him luck. They reassured Theo he'd come back in one piece, but Gabriel wasn't as convinced.

Once the Christmas tree was set up in the living room and trimmed with ornaments and goodwill, Katerina handed Theo the Christmas Angel to perform his annual duty so it could reign over the Conlon family holiday season. The possibility this moment could be Theo's last time placing it atop the tree was everyone's thought. The mood was too somber for carols or for offering and receiving gifts. Hugs were the best presents; love was still in the room.

Gabriel's duties at his office increased after Pearl Harbor. He determined which supply and troop trains arrived at port docks so that tanks, arms, soldiers and provisions could be loaded onto ships steaming across the oceans to far-flung battlefronts. His patriotism rarely wavered.

Three weeks after the quiet Christmas, Rose Conlon was never so afraid in her life. On a platform at Union Station in downtown Chicago, she watched her first born go off to war. She vented her anger at Gabriel whose responsibility was to make sure that Theo reached his destination on time and without interruption. Would he be as punctual about burying him too?

Both Gabriel and Rose pretended life was normal, if there was ever an accurate definition of what normal was.

They tried to keep their worry within the walls of their home. Katerina tended to Patricia as she finished high school and went off to college in Carbondale.

Gabriel purposely let work responsibilities distract him from a daily litany of what-if possibilities about Theo and his destiny. Rose did likewise while training nurses to handle the injuries of GIs sent home from battlefields and wondering if the next stretcher would carry her son, limbless or lifeless. She kept all anguish and sorrow outside the Conlon home, making it a fortress against despair and hopelessness.

At first, everyone in the house wrote to Theo at least once a week. Sometimes it was a brief note, other times a long letter, all addressed to APO San Francisco. By the second year of the war, they didn't know if the notes and letters ever arrived where Theo was, if they would ever know – which was better than revealing where he was and giving the enemy an advantage. Not knowing was knowing – and no news meant no telegram being delivered by a soldier in uniform. Rose's graying hair signaled her distress and sorrow.

D-Day gave hope for victory in Europe but Theo was somewhere in the South Pacific. Rose made sure her letters remained positive and uplifting. She didn't tell him that his grandmother Katerina had died suddenly and was buried with his grandfather in Wisconsin. Only good and happy news for Theo, she promised herself.

Rose wanted the house decorated early for Christmas that year, she placing the Christmas Angel on top of the tree this time by herself. She wrote a Christmas card to Theo, knowing it wouldn't get there in time or if it would even get there at all. The message in her card was more detailed than she intended, prompting her to continue her thoughts on a sheet of stationery paper.

Dearest Theo,

It's Christmas Eve and you are constantly on our mind. The Christmas Angel is looking down on me writing this card to you and no doubt it is looking down on you as well, wherever your somewhere is. Maybe it's remembering how you used to secure it at the top of the tree every year, your father first lifting you up as an infant to do so. Now you're a Marine fighting in the Pacific theater and your angel and family are hoping you are well and out of harm's way. Your Blue Star banner hangs in the front window.

Patricia is doing well in college and is dating a dental student. She says he's swell which is all right with Dad and me. He makes her happy but he may be enlisting soon in the Army. Dad continues to do his part for the war effort, collecting for the paper drive, buying Liberty Bonds and planning his next victory garden for this spring. Gas rationing keeps us at home except to drive to work but we do go to the picture show on Saturday to see the newsreels and learn about the war. It keeps us informed and hopeful that it all will end soon.

I am teaching young nurses to administer injections and how to tend to new patients. I always think about their families being proud of their sons and fathers and brothers but being thankful they're alive. We pray for you every Sunday at church and every day at home. We can only trust in God for your safe and healthy return.

Grandma Katie was making bandages for the American Red Cross but had to stop because of her arthritis. Aunt Lena retired from the brewery and helps with paperwork at a naval shipyard where Isabella is a welder.

I have baked my panettone for Christmas morning. I was able to find enough eggs and flour. I may have to stop, Theo. I hear carolers coming up the front walk.

I'm back writing to you. We invited the carolers in for hot chocolate and something more vigorous. When they left, an impromptu snowball fight broke out. The fathers acted more like children than the actual youngsters. I was glad to see that. We need to keep the Christmas spirit alive and home life as normal as possible, even with the heartache and heartbreak. The Lord himself will take care.

You will get this note sometime in the spring, I suspect, and maybe the war will be over by then. I pray you will be home and you won't even need to read this news from here. You can see it for yourself.

Dad joins me in sending you our love. Merry Christmas, my precious Theodore, my gift of God.

All my love,

Mother

Two atomic bombs ended the war. Theo telephoned he was alive and well, but didn't know when he would be discharged. He told his mother all he wanted to do when he got home was to hear birds sing in the early morning as the sun came up.

Theo's troop ship arrived in San Francisco by mid-December and he was home by Christmas. He first surprised his parents by joining carolers at their front door then afterward, he drove with his father to get the tree which Gabriel had set aside, the last one at the VFW Christmas tree lot. With people so happy the war was over, every fir and spruce had been sold. Glad and relieved to be together again, the Conlon family decorated their home for Christmas with garlands and ribbons, Theo once again placing the Christmas Angel atop the tree. Rose Conlon couldn't stop crying.

Theo stayed in Chicago to finish his degree at Lake Forest College under the GI Bill. He read a newspaper article about a local war hero honored for his gallantry at Anzio named Reginald Washington who recently joined the Chicago Fire Department and said that his career in firefighting began with a toy fire truck he was given as a gift one Christmas many years ago.

During his last semester of college, Theo received a letter from Albert Robbins saying he would soon graduate from Columbia University in New York City and be working in his father's investment firm. He wrote Theo he too would have a job waiting for him on Wall Street, if he wanted it.

Theo wanted it. After he accepted Albert's offer, his parents once again waved good-bye to their son on a platform at Union Station, but this time Rose's tears were happy ones.

Theo rode the 20th Century Limited to New York, his father reserving him a Pullman berth. Once in Manhattan, the two college friends were roommates again, this time on the Upper East Side.

After getting settled, Theo and Albert double-dated for an evening of a Broadway musical followed by a late dinner uptown. Albert fixed up Theo with his sister Susan who in turn fixed up her brother with a fellow legal secretary, Alicia Lawson.

At the end of the evening, the four of them gathered outside the Barbizon Hotel when, in a question intended for Susan, Theo asked, "Would you mind if I called on you?" But it was Alicia who answered him, "Yes, that would be fine."

Six months later, Theo and Alicia eloped to Elkton, Maryland.

Christmas Eighty-Six

The Conlon newlyweds hosted their first Christmas Eve in a cramped walk-up apartment not far from Grand Central Station, one that offered a glimpse of the East River, but only if a curtain was parted enough to reveal boat traffic. Friends from work, as well as Albert Robbins and his sister Susan, joined the gathering, Susan revealing to Alicia that their family surname was originally Rabinowitz, to which Alicia answered, "That's perfect. After all, Christmas celebrates the birth of a Jew."

Later that night, Gabriel and Rose telephoned from Illinois to say their house felt lonely, especially with Patricia spending the holidays with her new boyfriend's family in Ohio. Theo said he and Alicia would do the same the next day with Alicia's family in Connecticut. When Gabriel remarked it had been he who placed the Christmas Angel atop the tree that year, Theo said no matter where anyone in the family was, the Christmas Angel would send out its Christmas spirit in search of a Christmas miracle.

Remembering what he said to his father, Theo was convinced the miracle happened nine months later when his and Alicia's daughter was born, tempting Theo to name her Gloria since she was an "angel from on high." However, Alicia preferred the baby be named for her two grandmothers, Malinda Rose, but agreed with Theo she should be called Lindy. Albert and Susan Robbins warmly accepted their offer to be her godparents.

With Lindy spending her first weeks in a repurposed dresser drawer, Theo signed a mortgage for a two-story, wood-frame house near his in-laws. As much as he enjoyed the benefits of living in Manhattan, city Christmases weren't ones Theo cherished. Different wasn't necessarily better.

Although it was years later, Theo tried to relive his childhood holidays but time had moved on. When Lindy was nine, her grandmother Rose was diagnosed with breast cancer and Theo flew his family to Illinois for his mother's last Christmas. Together, Lindy and Rose placed the Christmas Angel on top of the tree. The Christmases Theo cherished were his once again.

Lindy was intrigued by the words and number engraved on the Christmas Angel. Theo explained he knew nothing beyond the inscription being someone's name and a year. He said he would solve the mystery someday but for now, the Christmas Angel was perfect where it was. Lindy replied, "Maybe Franz Hartmann carved the angel in 1872."

"Maybe," her father said. "And maybe one day we will know the answer."

That Christmas, Lindy hadn't brought anything with her on the plane to give her grandparents, ultimately only having herself to give. While she couldn't wrap her heart in a bow, she did find something in a bedroom closet.

Christmas morning, Lindy presented her grandparents with a wrapped cardboard shoebox. However, they were confused upon unwrapping it then lifting off its lid to find it empty. Smiling, Lindy explained, "It's filled to the top with all my hugs and kisses."

Rose Conlon succumbed at home to cancer the following summer and Gabriel died there nine years later of an aneurysm, while Lindy was in college. Following their father's funeral, Patricia and Theo sorted and boxed family items and mementoes. Patricia reasoned she didn't want the Christmas Angel since her home and furnishings were modern and sleek while the Christmas Angel was old, dated and had its time. "Just like all of us, Theo," she said. "I know you will give it a good home. Or you can return it to Franz Hartmann."

Theo packed the Christmas Angel securely in Lindy's cardboard shoebox and said he'd hold onto it himself during the flight home. Family tradition and its sentiment had helped get him through one war. Perhaps it would get the family through another one, the being fought in Southeast Asia.

In college, Lindy demonstrated against American involvement in Vietnam and wore a tie-dye shirt and blue jeans to emphasize her politics. She said her father and grandfather fought in wars with a moral purpose, saying technology, determination and a rightful cause couldn't achieve a desired victory in disease-infested jungles. "Why, Dad? Is it worth it?" she asked.

"Yes, it's worth it. Giving all to everything is always worth it."

"What's the 'it,' Dad?"

"Whatever you want 'it' to be, Lindy. Your choice, your life."

Before her grandfather's funeral, Lindy wrote a political science paper about her thoughts on the Fourth of July.

"Happy birthday, America. You are a nation that will never be happy with itself. Whether it was Aaron Burr versus Alexander Hamilton, ending slavery and accepting personal responsibility, or having both its soldiers and students die because of Vietnam, America will always have one citizen wanting to exert power over another citizen. Your goals and ideologies disregard the selfishness of human nature. Yes, all men are created equal, but after that, everyone

```
is on their own. And
everyone, no exceptions,
wants something given to
them without earning it,
resulting in the squalor
of your bankrupt treasury
and unattainable founding
principles. So happy
birthday, America, where
no one is happy."
```

Lindy didn't like that she had to write about her anger. When Alicia read Lindy's diatribe, she suggested to her daughter that sometimes people need to be like a candy store. "Offer something people want to enjoy and still be sweet."

Lindy decided she'd be the only one who could make herself happy, since no one person and no one thing could do it for her. She was tired of rage. She didn't like what it did to her. She wanted what was bad in society to be good and what was good in society to be better. "Dad, I keep asking 'what if' and never getting an answer."

"The answer will come from inside you, Lindy, and not anywhere else," he said. "When you think you are more than you are, you will become so."

Lindy and her parents landed at JFK Airport and headed through the terminal toward an exit, carrying luggage and the Christmas Angel in its shoebox. She heard music and recognized the lyrics of a Scott McKenzie song about going to San Francisco and being sure to wear some flowers in your hair because you're gonna meet some gentle people there.

A bearded and ponytailed young man sat cross-legged with a battery-operated record player on the floor near the baggage carousel. On the back of his Army field jacket was embroidered "When I die, I'm going to heaven because I've served my time in hell. Vietnam."

When Lindy passed him, they flashed each other the peace sign. She continued toward the exit when she heard someone yell at him, "Baby killer."

Lindy looked back to see the veteran's face as he sang the song to himself – alone, rejected, shunned, despised – through no fault of his own – but still singing through his tears.

During the ride home to Connecticut, Lindy sat silent in the backseat, holding the Christmas Angel on her lap. She couldn't forget the veteran's eyes. "That wasn't right, Dad. That soldier didn't have a choice. Only he knows what happened. Who are we to judge? He has to live with what was done to him."

"Or with what he did to himself," Alicia said. "Everyone has a life to live, Lindy. I'm not telling you something you don't already know. But it all happens while we seek our own truth about ourselves. The fortunate ones find it. You'll find yours, Lindy, but it may take some time. And that soldier will too."

Lindy stared at the Christmas Angel. "All I know is I wanted to hold him and to tell him everything was going to be all right."

She asked her parents if she could join them at church that Sunday. It had been years since she felt a need to pray, but she said she needed to do so now for that soldier, and for the nation he had served so honorably.

Perhaps both would find grace and forgiveness, she thought. And hope for the future.

She would include herself in those prayers.

Christmas
One Hundred

L indy Conlon finished graduate school in social work and psychology at NYU, then found a consulting job in Manhattan, as well as a studio apartment in Brooklyn. When her father retired early from Wall Street to volunteer for local groups and charities at home, he told Lindy that knowing all the bridges and tunnels in and out of Manhattan didn't make him feel any more of a New Yorker than before. They merely provided him with a daily means to escape urban hubris – until the day he caught his final 5:15 train to Darien.

Single and in her late twenties, Lindy sought trust and loyalty in a romantic relationship, all of which had eluded her so far. Realizing city life made her jaded, skewed and judgmental, she sought a distraction to regain her empathy, compassion and understanding. She needed Christmas in July, a desire which made her think of one thing.

Five months later, Lindy took the 5:15 from Grand Central to Darien where Theo met her at the station. Both were excited to see each other. Theo had his daughter home to help ready the house for Christmas – and Lindy was anxious to share a discovery she made: the identity of Franz Hartmann.

"Dad, it's quite a few names. With some great stories. The Hartmans wound up in New York and I think one of them lives a couple of hours from here. I put together their family tree for the fun of it. Like any family, they've got some scoundrels but also a lot of neat people in it."

After dinner, Alicia made eggnog while Lindy, Theo and she trimmed the tree with garlands, ornaments and the Christmas Angel on top. Lindy unfolded a sketch of a genealogical table in front of the Christmas Angel, nodding toward it. "This is all because of you."

Lindy said at first, she felt like a snoop, except she reasoned she was also getting to know people with whom she shared something special. She began her search for Franz Hartmann in the New York Public Library on Fifth Avenue, pouring over census records, local histories, family files, biographies, genealogies and microfilms. In a volume of passenger lists from the Palatinate, she found Franz Hartmann aged 10 and his parents Johann Hartmann aged 34 and Marie Luise Hartmann aged 32 immigrating on the ship *Valkyrie*, last of Rotterdam, in the year 1872. The name and date confirmed the engraved inscription at the base of the Christmas Angel.

An index of the 1880 U.S. Federal Census had two Franz Hartmanns, several Francis Hartmanns and more than forty Frank Hartmans throughout the American Midwest, from Ohio to Iowa, from Pennsylvania to Colorado. But only three were born in Germany and one of them was living in Denver. It bore the excised names of Johann and Franz Hartmann corrected to John and

Frank Hartman. A microfilm verified the information which noted that their birthplace of Bavaria had been changed to Missouri.

As far as Lindy was concerned, answers to questions generated during her research led to more questions to be answered.

Then she found what she sought: the same census record listed members of the Hartman household, including Patrick Conlon and Katerina Wolters. "Dad, I found your grandparents living with Franz Hartmann. We found him. We found the Christmas Angel."

Lindy's excitement became infectious. She pointed to the genealogical chart, "I needed to know more, especially about what happened to this family. I wanted to know how things might have been different for the Christmas Angel if it hadn't been with us for one hundred years."

Her research determined that Frank Hartman had moved with his wife Helen and their two sons from Manhattan to Tarrytown, New York, according to the 1900 U.S. Federal Census. A volume with marriage records for New York City showed Frank Hartman was married there to Helen Armstrong in 1888. Lindy said a librarian guided her to a published genealogy of the Armstrong family where she found Helen Armstrong Hartman's line of descent from an Armstrong immigrant to Boston in 1640 which contained names of ancestors who sailed on the *Mayflower*, fought in the Revolutionary War, and served in every American war through the Great War. Lindy noted that Helen's mother had written an article about her daughter's family.

Lindy then told her parents, "Frank Hartman went to college and worked in a customs house in downtown Manhattan with Herman Melville who wrote *Moby-Dick*. He and Helen had two sons: Matthew born in 1891 and William in 1894, both in New York City. And then they moved to Tarrytown. Both sons enlisted in World War I. William Hartman was wounded in the Argonne Forest and died later of his injuries. After the war, the older brother Matthew married a milliner from Bedford, New York named Rebecca Townsend who was from a pacifist Quaker family. Matthew became a corporate lawyer in Manhattan and they had three children: William Townsend Hartman, Robert Armstrong Hartman, and Georgiana Purcell Hartman."

"That's wonderful, Lindy," said Alicia. "We should try to contact them."

"There's more, Mom. I found the obituary in *The Times* for Matthew Hartman from nine years ago. It was on microfilm. It mentioned he was predeceased by his wife and by a son who died during D-Day, but it also named his son and daughter who survived, along with the names of grandchildren. At the time, William Townsend Hartman was a college professor who lived in eastern Pennsylvania with his wife and son." Lindy then asked, "What do I do now?"

"Call him up," said Theo. "See if he's still there. He's got to be about my age. I wonder if his father and uncle fought alongside my father and uncle during World War I."

"Only one way to find that out," said Alicia. "Call him up."

Theo called long distance information, scribbled a phone number on a pad and dialed. "Hello. Is this William Hartman?... I am Theodore Conlon and I believe we have something that belonged to your family a long time ago."

For the next hour, Bill Hartman and Theo Conlon shared stories. Bill related how his grandfather told him about the wooden angel and how it had been lost. He even posssesed a tintype of Opa, the man who carved it, his great, great grandfather, Franz Friedrich Hartmann. Bill spoke about being with his brother on D-Day and how history repeated itself when he died in a French hospital days later and then how Bill married his brother's girlfriend after the war was over, saying they fell in love while sharing a mutual sorrow. "Grief is love that has nowhere to go," said Bill. "Sarah and I gave it a place to go."

Bill mentioned he and Sarah named their son Robert for his brother and that he had lived in California for ten years but recently returned to New York City to work for Doctors Without Borders. Theo gave Bill their telephone number to give to his son. "I am sure Rob would love to meet you," said Bill. "He'll be there in your area for Christmas. Sarah and I fly to Florida tomorrow to be with my sister and her husband. A sandy beach is our version of a white Christmas. But Rob plans to ski in Vermont over the holidays. I'm sure you can expect a call from him. He's not shy. Trust me."

Alicia and Lindy had overheard the conversation on an extension phone. Alicia said, "He's more than welcome to come by. We're here. No one should ever be alone at Christmas."

Rob Hartman called the Conlons the next morning, Christmas Eve. He said he'd like to drive out to meet them but it'd have to be a quick visit since he wanted to be in Vermont that evening. Three hours later, he walked toward the front door of the Conlon home wearing a parka, wool hat and snow boots.

Lindy opened the door before he could ring the bell. She knew him. She had seen his face before. Years before. Maybe ten or more years ago. She could never forget his eyes. He had since shaved his beard and cut his hair. But the eyes were the same. They were most definitely his. She was carrying the Christmas Angel through the baggage claim area at JFK Airport. He had worn an Army field jacket with an outline of Vietnam on the back. He was sitting cross-legged on the floor of the terminal, in front of a portable record player, listening to a song play over-and-over again.

Rob sank into her eyes. "I know you."

"Did you ever make it to San Francisco?"

"Yes. It changed my life."

"Come in, please."

He thanked her and took off his wool hat as he entered. "I knew I would see you again. You were carrying a wooden angel in a shoebox."

"It's right there." She pointed to the top of the Christmas tree. "There's your angel."

Rob corrected her. "Our angel," then he mumbled, "And it's not the only angel in the room."

But she hadn't heard him. "Hi. My name is Lindy."

"Hi. I'm Rob."

Rob eventually made it to Vermont, but it would be a year-and-a-half later. Malinda Rose Conlon was married to Robert Armstrong Hartman II under a two-hundred-year-old Norway spruce at the crest of a sun-lit hilltop meadow. Suspended above them on a branch as they pledged their love and devotion to each other was the Christmas Angel.

Christmas
One Hundred Fifty

Rob Hartman was speechless
holding the Christmas Angel
for the first time, unable to describe
the depth of the moment, his thoughts
insufficient and useless to the wonder of
touching something created so lovingly
by the hands of his great, great, great
grandfather.

Rob knew well as he held it, that
the Christmas Angel had witnessed the
refrains of hundreds of carols sung under
its oak wings, the reunion of soldiers

returning home from war, and the countless gasps of children awestruck by the handiwork of Santa's elves. He didn't know it had also been singed when a candleholder with a clay-ball counterweight shifted on a bough, that it had felt the heat of the first electric lightbulbs to grace pine branches below its whittled robe, smelled a hand-strung popcorn-and-berry pioneer garland draped near its wings, and had winked back at tinsel sparkling off its beseeching hands.

Rob kept staring at something he considered to be almost divinely inspired, it having celebrated more than one hundred Christmases, and would, God willing, celebrate one hundred, two hundred more. In that moment, and with a woman beside him who knew him at his worst and now saw him at his best, Rob Hartman cried at finding the part of his soul he thought had long gone missing.

Lindy then did something she had wanted to do when she first saw him all those years ago. She held him close and told him everything would be all right.

Rob breathed deep and thanked her. She then helped him replace the Christmas Angel atop the tree, just as the first wave of neighbors and friends arrived at the front door, entering with snow on their coats and smiles on their faces, everyone bearing glad tidings of comfort, joy, food, cheer and song.

Hours later, guests and visitors left the Conlon home with empty platters, casserole dishes, instrument cases, pie tins, and Christmas gift bags of small homemade loaves and jars of jellies Alicia had made. In their wake, wrapped and ribboned presents lingered under the tree while plates of Christmas cookies and gingerbread men adorned the dining table. Friends trudged home through snow and wind, their hearts blessed by another Conlon family Christmas Eve, warm with memories of off-key singing, inescapable laughter, and love in the room.

Rob and Lindy had no Christmas gifts to offer each other except to give of themselves to one another. They stayed up all night that Christmas Eve talking and listening, listening and talking, waiting for Santa Claus to wobble down the chimney and avoid embers in the fireplace. By dawn, they surrendered to the demands of sleep as Rob laid his head against the back of the sofa and Lindy used Rob's chest for a pillow. All the while, the Christmas Angel watched over them, embracing and protecting.

In the morning, Rob and Lindy were alone near the Christmas tree and discovered they were under a sprig of mistletoe. Without hesitation, they kissed – and time stopped. They didn't need to go anywhere else; their search was over. "Hold me," each revealed wordlessly to the other, "I'm yours."

Rob Hartman said his Christmas with the Conlons was his best since he was a little kid and had raced downstairs Christmas morning in his pajamas to discover a big-boy, fat-tire, two-wheel bicycle under the tree. Theo and Alicia later described their son-in-law as the man who came for Christmas and never left.

Rob and Lindy Hartman eventually settled in the village of Castle Hills, New York about an hour north of her parents where their four children were born. The new parents thought of naming their first son Franz but knew that name belonged elsewhere so he was christened James. Two years later, Thomas arrived, followed in another two years by the twins Abigail and Hannah.

For them, Castle Hills was ideal, a town which welcomed everyone and where no one locked their doors, a sanctuary surrounded by the Americana of a nation confident and secure in its heritage and spiritual values, ones based on faith, trust, country, duty, respect and eternal hope. The village was safe and secure, perfect to raise a family which would give of itself to each other and to others.

At Christmastime, brightly lit giant snowflakes were strewn among spruce and pine trees in the town park while festive twinkle lights wrapped the support posts and roof of a gazebo, ringed streetlamps at the edge of a skating pond, and draped sides of a footbridge spanning a snow-covered brook. A menorah and a crescent-moon-and-star joined a Christmas tree by the gazebo to celebrate Abrahamic traditions shared during the holiday season by local citizenry.

Once the twins were in kindergarten, Lindy returned to college to earn a teaching degree while Rob traveled often for Doctors Without Borders, being reluctant to retire after forty years. His military training helped him coordinate rescue-and-recovery operations for natural and man-made disasters around the world: floods, earthquakes, tsunamis, landslides, avalanches and war zones. He rejected an offer with a federal disaster relief agency because he refused to move his family to Washington, D.C.

Rob and Lindy maintained that every child should grow up in a small town, especially at Christmastime. However, such solid serenity did not mean grief and fear wouldn't interfere, especially when risk and chance were required for people to aspire toward success and to achieve goals. Their life together became balanced like a Janus mask: half tragedy and half comedy.

After their wedding, the new Mr. and Mrs. Robert Hartman also married holiday traditions of both families: raise up the youngest child to place the Christmas Angel atop the tree; serve Fish House Punch to honor an Armstrong ancestor who crossed the Delaware River with George Washington on Christmas Day 1776; and host a Christmas Eve open house of friends and neighbors, especially those who might be alone that night.

Included too were Lindy and Rob's shared memories and experiences of the holidays, gathered over their forty-plus years in Castle Hills. There was the time that three Santas showed up in costume at the end of a Christmas concert at the library (a Catholic, a Jew and a Hindu)...

or the time the head of the Baby Jesus doll featured in the church Christmas pageant rolled from the chancel into a front pew... or when the high school football team encircled the town in candle luminaria so the village shined for its annual winter walk... as well as the time the Hartman family dressed as the Cratchits from *A Christmas Carol* for the town holiday parade and both twins stepped in fresh poop deposited in the middle of the street, courtesy of a Belgian horse in front of them pulling an elves-filled wagon.

Then there was the time when the Hartman kids knocked over the Christmas tree and the Christmas Angel flew onto the sofa for a safe landing... and when all the bright lights in the park went on all at once during the annual holiday lighting ceremony and short-circuited... or when a few carolers along Main Street imbibed too much Christmas cheer. There was also the time when the Christmas tree flew off the roof of the car on its way home and into a snowbank on the side of the road... and when Lindy handknit all the family's Christmas stockings for the mantelpiece... or when Thomas and his long-time partner

Zander announced their engagement at Christmas Day dinner... or most recently when Rob and Lindy helped their first grandchild Alonso place the Christmas Angel atop their Christmas tree.

But their fun and laughter didn't exist without pain and sorrow. Family tragedies and sadness interceded, personally as well as nationally. The Hartmans and America both endured lethal pandemics, terrorist attacks, financial crises and political scandals. Alicia Conlon was killed in an automobile accident, with Theo literally dying of a broken heart months later due to cardiac arrest. Several years afterward, Rob's parents passed on, Bill from leukemia and Sarah from heart disease.

Rob likened such cycles of life to the days before and after Christmas. Once "Auld Lang Syne" was sung on New Year's Eve and the church calendar transited into Epiphany, glass balls and precious mementos were packed away before the tree shed the bulk of its pine needles and was carried outside, its purpose now past, even if it was before its time. The Christmas Angel was boxed and shelved, to await the following December when it would reign yet again over a young, vibrant fir or spruce or pine, glad to be reunited with old ornaments and garlands while greeting cards were written and received, smells of roast beef and apple pie wafted from the oven, evergreen boughs enhanced wreaths and doorways, thoughtful presents were wrapped and beribboned, and families posed for photographs and selfies by the Christmas tree in matching pajamas or dressed in stylish clothes before a candlelight service or costumed as Nativity figures for a church pageant.

And as happened each year, God willing, the Christmas Angel welcomed newly crafted decorations hung below it to inspire and create fresh memories, or to watch over an electric train circling the tree skirt or a tricycle with a large red bow sitting in anticipation of its years ahead as a child's best friend. From the front window of the Hartman home, the Christmas Angel could observe the reunions of loved ones arriving with presents and hearing shouts of "Grandma, let me show you what Santa Claus brought me."

The Christmas Angel had witnessed it all and more, since Opa presented it to ten-year-old Franz Hartmann to bring to America. No, Opa, Franz did not forget. And neither did anyone else; no one forgot that the meaning of Christmas was giving of oneself to others from deep within.

With the marriage of James Hartman to his college sweetheart Valentina Garza and the birth of Alonso, Lindy and Rob reassessed their past and pondered their future. They used to cry at the ending of *It's A Wonderful Life* not because they were happy for the Bailey family and Clarence Odbody, but because they were happy for themselves and each other. Reel life was real life. Life imitated art. They had lived the movie in their love of family, devotion to community, and selfless hospitality to friends and strangers during all seasons, but especially Christmastime.

The Christmas Angel had caused it all. Without its spirit, Lindy and Rob knew there would have been no them. With their good fortune and blessings, they realized every person and every family had a Christmas Angel, maybe not one made of Bavarian oak which had been passed down for generations, but everyone possessed a cherished tradition or symbol to embody a universal

Christmas Spirit, a personal assurance that miracles can and do happen and that they are eternal.

For them, the final words in a letter Lindy found after her father died said everything. He had written to his parents during the last Christmas of World War II. The letter was on lined notebook paper and appeared to have been written with a pencil stub on an Army helmet. It was dated 24 December 1944, Somewhere in the South Pacific:

And say Merry Christmas to the Christmas Angel for me. Tell it I am sorry not to place it on top of the tree again this year, but that I hope to be home next Christmas. In the meantime, I know it'll continue to watch over everyone and embrace and protect us.

When I was a young boy, I asked Grandma Katie if our Christmas Angel was real. She said if I wanted it to be real, then it was. She told me that one of its wings was faith and the other wing was hope, but that *what made it soar among the heavens was love. She said that whenever charity was in my heart, the angel was real.*

This Christmas and every Christmas, the angel is real.

I love you all.

Theo

Lindy finished reading the letter to Rob and returned it to the shoebox. Once again, love transformed into memory – silent, endless, undeniable.

It was just the two of them now on Christmas Eve.

The house was decorated and readied for the family arriving tomorrow to open presents and to enjoy Christmas dinner. Gifts were wrapped, cookies were baked and the Christmas Angel was secure on a top bough. Embers faded in the fireplace as snow fell outside in the stillness.

Lindy and Rob turned off all the downstairs lights and started upstairs for bed.

Then a bright light went on in the living room. Both swore they saw it but wouldn't ever say anything to anyone because no one would ever believe them.

Atop the tree in the dark and quiet, the Christmas Angel glowed.

Edward L. Woodyard lives in Westchester County, New York with his wife, Nancy.

Three
Lions
Rampant